Little Quack and Baby Ducky

By Ward Smith

Illustrated by Tom Cooke

A GOLDEN BOOK • NEW YORK

Western Publishing Company, Inc., Racine, Wisconsin 53404

S0-BOT-321

Baby Ducky is Little Quack's favorite toy. Little Quack sleeps with Baby Ducky.

He eats with Baby Ducky.

He takes Baby Ducky everywhere he goes.

But one afternoon Little Quack cannot find
Baby Ducky. He cries, "Quack, quack, quack.
I want my Baby Ducky back!"

Little Quack's mother says, "Did you look in the toy box?"

Little Quack runs to the toy box. No Baby Ducky.

Mrs. Quack asks if Little Quack woke
up with Baby Ducky that morning.
"Yes!" says Little Quack. He runs and
looks in his bed. No Baby Ducky.
"Quack, quack, quack! I want my
Baby Ducky back!" cries Little Quack.

His mother tells him to look *under* the bed.
Little Quack gets down on his knees. He pokes
his head under the bed. No Baby Ducky.

"What did you do after you woke up?" asks Mrs. Quack.

"I ate breakfast," says Little Quack.

"That's right," says his mother.

Little Quack and his mother hurry to the kitchen. They look all over. No Baby Ducky.

"What did you do after breakfast?" Mrs. Quack
asks.

"I don't know," cries Little Quack.

"Think hard," says his mother.

"I know! I know! I played in the yard!" says
Little Quack.

Little Quack and his mother look in the yard.
But they do not find Baby Ducky.

Dennis Duck comes along. "Do you want to play?" he asks.

"No! I want my Baby Ducky! Do you know where he is?"

"Did you look in the sandbox?" asks Dennis.

Little Quack looks in the sandbox. No Baby Ducky.

"You went to Tulip's house this morning," says
Mrs. Quack. "Maybe you left Baby Ducky there."

Little Quack and Dennis go over to Tulip's house. "Have you seen my Baby Ducky?" asks Little Quack.

"No," says Tulip, "but you can come in and look."

Little Quack and Tulip look everywhere, but
they cannot find Baby Ducky.

Little Quack sees Tulip's brother, Skipper.
"Have you seen my Baby Ducky?" he asks.
"I saw you both at the playground today,"
answers Skipper.
"The playground!" shouts Little Quack. "Let's
go to the playground!"

In the playground Little Quack and his friends look by the swings. They look all around. But they do not find Baby Ducky.

They find their friend Sunflower instead. "Have you seen my Baby Ducky?" asks Little Quack.

"I saw Baby Ducky with you at the pond," says
Sunflower.

They all race to the pond. But there is no Baby
Ducky.

"Where is my Baby Ducky?" wails Little
Quack. "I want my Baby Ducky!"

Mrs. Quack comes to see if Little Quack has found Baby Ducky. She hugs Little Quack and thinks for a moment. "There is one more place to look," she says. "We went to the store today."

"Maybe *that's* where I left Baby Ducky!" says Little Quack.

Little Quack and his mother go to Mr. Rooster's grocery store.

"Have you seen my Baby Ducky?" Little Quack asks Mr. Rooster.

Mr. Rooster smiles. "Cock-a-doodle-doo, I have a rubber duck just for you!" he says.

Mr. Rooster hands Baby Ducky to Little Quack.
"Baby Ducky! Baby Ducky!" cries Little Quack.
Mr. Rooster says, "Cock-a-doodle-doo, Baby
Ducky sure missed you!"

Little Quack gives Baby Ducky a big hug and holds him tight all the way home.